NIGEL HINTON

On the Edge

For Sara

First published in 2014 in Great Britain by
Barrington Stoke Ltd
18 Walker Street, Edinburgh, EH3 7LP

www.barringtonstoke.co.uk

ISBN: 978-1-78112-309-6

Printed in China by Leo

Contents

Chapter 1
He's Coming to Get Us

Dillon was in the middle of a game of *Storm Fury* when the phone rang.

"Robbie – get the phone," he called.

"I'm reading," Robbie yelled back.

"I can't stop my game," Dillon shouted. "Get it!"

There was a groan, then Dillon heard his younger brother stomp down the stairs and answer the phone.

It was probably Mum checking that they were OK. Nan always came round to look after them in the holidays but she was ill. Mum had wanted to stay home but Dillon had said that would be stupid.

"Come on, Mum, you've got loads of work. Anyway, I'm 15 next week. Robbie's ten. It's not like we're little kids."

Mum hadn't been happy about it but she'd given in. So it was probably her on the phone, worried the house was on fire or something. She'd calm down when she heard Robbie.

Then a word cut through the noise of all the shooting on *Storm Fury*. The word was "Dad".

Dad?

Had Robbie really said that?

It couldn't be their dad on the phone. He wasn't allowed to contact them now. He wasn't even allowed within a mile of the house since he'd beaten Mum up so badly two years ago. Anyway he was still in that place, wasn't he? They wouldn't have let him out, would they? Would they?

Maybe Robbie had said 'Andy'. Or maybe he'd called Andy 'Dad' by mistake. Dillon had done that a couple of times. Andy had been seeing more and more of Mum and next month he would be moving in with them. And he was a nice guy so it was easy to slip up and call him 'Dad'. Andy always laughed when that happened but you could see he was pleased.

But Robbie wouldn't make that mistake. He didn't dislike Andy but he wasn't very happy about him living with them. Robbie still hoped that Dad would come back.

"He's our real dad," Robbie always said when Mum couldn't hear them.

That was probably because Robbie was younger than Dillon and couldn't really remember all the things that had happened – the rows, the fights, the mad bursts of temper. Plus, Robbie was Dad's favourite and he never hit him, not the way he hit Dillon and Mum.

Even when Dillon tried to tell Robbie what Dad was like, Robbie always shook his head. "I don't care, he's our real dad."

It was true. He was their real dad. And, nice as Andy was, he could never take Dad's place. Even Dillon knew that, deep down.

Dillon clicked PAUSE on *Storm Fury*. Robbie wasn't saying anything. He must be listening. Then there were a couple of short mumbles. Then the word "OK".

A moment later Robbie came into the room. He had a big smile on his face and he was almost shaking with excitement.

"That was Dad!"

"Our dad?" Dillon asked. Lame question.

"Of course our dad."

"What did he want?"

"He's coming to get us."

Chapter 2
It's Him

"What do you mean – Dad's coming to get us?" Dillon asked.

"He wants to take us on holiday for a couple of days." Robbie was beaming.

"What did you tell him?"

"I said OK."

"Are you stupid?" Dillon shouted. "He's not supposed to see us. There's a restraining order."

"He said Mum said it was OK."

"He's lying," Dillon said. "Mum would never let him take us away."

Gunshots rang out.

Dillon's finger had slipped off the PAUSE button on *Storm Fury*. He hit OFF on the TV remote and picked up his mobile. He scrolled to Mum's number and pressed CALL. Ten rings, but she still didn't answer. "Come on," he said. "Pick up!"

Then Dillon realised he could hear a phone ringing in the house. He ran into the kitchen. The ringing was coming from a phone on the worktop.

A chill ran down his back.

It was Mum's phone. She'd left it plugged in to charge. And Dillon didn't have the number of her office.

What about Nan? He couldn't ring her – she was ill and might be in bed asleep. Andy? No, he couldn't ask Andy to come and sort out Dad.

Dillon ran back into the living room.

"Did Dad say how long he'd be?" he asked.

"A couple of minutes," Robbie said.

Could they leave the house? Grab their bikes and go into town? It was probably too late. Best to stay here. Hide upstairs and not answer the door.

Dillon grabbed Robbie by the shoulders and pushed him towards the stairs.

"Let me go," Robbie said. "What are you doing?"

"We're going up to my room."

"Why?"

"So he can't see us. We'll just wait until he goes away."

"But it's Dad, Dill!"

Dillon kept pushing Robbie up the stairs, but at the top Robbie ducked and tried to break free.

"I want to see Dad! I want to go on holiday with him!"

"Robbie, listen," Dillon began. "Dad's ..."

What could he say? Dad's violent? Dad's dangerous?

"Remember when he hit Mum?" he asked, in the end.

"He said he was sorry," Robbie said.

"He broke her arm, Robbie. He knocked two teeth out. He's got a temper, he's been in –"

The doorbell rang.

"It's him!" Robbie said.

Dillon turned to open his bedroom door and Robbie broke out of his grasp and ran down the stairs.

By the time Dillon caught up with him, Robbie was opening the front door. Dillon tried to shut it again but a big army boot slid into the gap and wedged it open. He kept pushing but the force from the other side was too strong. Bit by bit, the front door opened.

It was no use struggling. Dillon let go and stepped back.

The door swung open and there was Dad.

Chapter 3
Cross My Heart and Hope to Die

Dad was dressed in combat gear, as if he'd never left the army. His face was tanned, which made the scar on his cheek look whiter than ever. He was proud of that scar. He'd got it from a piece of shrapnel when he was fighting in the Middle East.

There was a long moment as they looked at him and he looked at them. Dillon could hear Robbie take a deep breath. Waiting. Unsure.

Then Dad smiled a big, big smile. The kind of smile Dillon remembered from when he was a little kid. A big, open smile that warmed you like the sun coming out from behind the clouds. And Dillon couldn't help it – he smiled back. A big silly grin.

Robbie jumped up and threw his arms round Dad's neck, just like he used to in the old days. Robbie had grown a lot in the last couple of years but when Dad lifted him up in his massive arms, Robbie still looked like a little kid.

Dillon had forgotten how big Dad was – tall and strong. His arms and shoulders were thick with muscle and his hands looked huge on Robbie's back. He had shaved his hair very short and he had a tattoo just above his right ear. A word. Dillon couldn't see what it said.

"Oh Robbo, Robbo – it's so good to see you," Dad said. "Missed me?"

Robbie nodded and buried his face in Dad's neck.

"Me too, little man. Me too. But we can be together now. Everything's OK again."

He lowered Robbie to the ground and ruffled his hair. Then he looked at Dillon.

"Something the matter with that front door. It's sticking."

Dillon's heart was beating fast and he realised that he was holding his breath. Would Dad be angry? Would he fall into one of his bad moods because Dillon had tried to stop him getting in?

Then Dad winked and smiled again.

"It's OK, Dill. I understand. So, you gonna say hello or not?"

Dillon stepped forward and held out his hand.

"Don't I get a hug?" Dad asked. "Or are you too grown up now?"

Dad opened his arms and pulled him into a hug. Held him tight. Kissed the top of his head. And Dillon felt weak. It was so good, Dad stroking his back as if he really loved him.

"I've thought about you two every single day," Dad said. "It was like a big pain in my heart. All I could think about was seeing my boys."

Dad let go of Dillon and looked at him with tears in his blue eyes.

"And here you are, my little monkeys," Dad said. "And I want to say sorry for what I did. Sorry you've had to grow up without your dad. Sorry I was such a dipstick. But that's going to change. I'm always going to be here for you now. I've got my own place, and you can visit anytime you want."

"I thought you were still ..." Dillon said, and then didn't know how to go on.

"Locked up in St Mary's?" Dad said. "You can say it, Dill. I admit it – I was ill. Nuts. I had to be locked up. There's no shame in that. I needed help. But I'm better now so they let me out. Look at me. I'm right as rain. Your mum could see that – that's why she said it would be OK to let me take you away for a couple of days."

"She didn't tell us," Robbie said.

"Only just seen her, haven't I?" Dad said. "I dropped into the office for a chat. In fact, she was the one who came up with the idea. 'Why not take the boys away for a couple of days,' she said. 'They'd love a little trip. Take them to that place where we used to go for holidays – Gardle

Head.' Of course, I jumped at the chance. I've got my motor outside, all ready to go."

"Now?" Robbie asked.

"Yep," Dad said. "Just think we can be up there in about five or six hours. Sleep out under the stars. Light a bonfire. Barbecue some sausages. Eat them looking at the sea. Just us. Together. What d'you say?"

"Yeah!" Robbie said.

"That's my boy! Dill?"

Dillon wanted to believe him. He wanted to believe that Mum had said it was OK. He wanted to believe that Dad had changed.

Now Dillon had seen Dad again like this, he realised just how much he'd missed him. For two years he'd told himself that Dad was just a bully and all that. But he seemed so different now. So warm. Smiling. No doubt about it, he had changed. And, deep down, Dillon knew he still loved Dad. Still needed him. Andy was great, but Andy could never make him feel like this.

But ... was it really all OK?

"Are you sure Mum said we could go?" he asked.

"Cross my heart and hope to die," Dad said. "I tell you what, we'll drop by her office on the way and you can ask her yourself. OK?"

Dillon hesitated a moment. It was like being caught up in a whirlwind. One minute he'd been playing *Storm Fury*, and then – this. A trip with the man who had scared him so much in the past. But he seemed like a completely different man now. Like a real dad.

Dillon nodded. "OK."

Chapter 4
Just in Case

"OK, let's go," Dad said. He rubbed his hands together.

"Don't we need to pack first?" Dillon asked.

"You won't need anything," Dad replied.

"What? How long are we going for?"

A strange look flickered across Dad's face, as if he'd had a stab of pain. Then the smile was back. "Three or four days," he said. "We'll see how it goes. Yeah, you're right – nip up and grab some pants and stuff and something warm. And bring your sleeping bags. It can get chilly up on those cliffs."

Dillon ran upstairs, followed by Robbie. He went into his bedroom and pulled his sports bag out from under his bed. He stuffed some pants and socks and a couple of shirts inside, then added a hoodie in case it got cold.

"Don't forget your toothbrush!" Dad called from downstairs.

"OK," Dillon shouted. "Robbie – toothbrush!"

They both went into the bathroom and grabbed their washing things. They looked at each other and they couldn't help laughing – suddenly this all seemed like a great adventure.

"Beat you downstairs," Robbie said as he ran out of the bathroom.

As Dillon picked up his bag he looked out of the window. A big black 4x4 was parked outside the house. There were no other cars nearby. The 4x4 must be Dad's. He looked at the number plate – it was the latest model. Wow! It was going to be so great to drive up to Gardle Head in that.

Dillon was about to race downstairs when a sudden doubt flickered in his mind. That car must have cost a fortune. Where had Dad got the money? It would have cost a lot even to hire it. Had Dad got a job now? Where was he living? Had he really gone to see Mum? Had she really said it was OK to take Robbie and Dillon away?

Dillon wanted it to be true. He wanted everything to be good between Mum and Dad. And Dad had said they were going to stop at Mum's office, so it must be true.

But just in case it wasn't ...

Dillon picked up a pencil and ripped a page out of a notebook. He wrote down the number of the car. And under that he wrote, 'Gone to Gardle Head with Dad'.

Just in case.

Dillon put the piece of paper on his bed, picked up his bag and ran downstairs.

"Beat you!" Robbie said, with a grin. He was wearing his combat jacket – just like Dad. Dillon laughed and ruffled Robbie's hair. It was great to see him so happy.

Dad opened the front door.

"Right, here we go," he said. "Like the old days. Me and my boys."

They stepped outside, then Dad stopped and held out the car key to Dillon. "You open it," he said. "I'd better have a quick pee before we go. And you forgot the sleeping bags. Are they still in the cupboard under the stairs? I'll fetch them."

Dillon took the key and watched as Dad went back into the house.

"Come on," Robbie said, "I want to see the car."

They ran out to the street and stopped next to the gleaming 4x4. It looked even better close up. It was a top of the range model and Dillon couldn't help smiling as he held out the key and unlocked the doors.

"It's better than Andy's old banger," Robbie said. "Dad says I can sit in the front."

Dillon didn't argue. Robbie always got car sick in the back and anyway, there would be more room to stretch out there. He put their two bags in the boot. There was a cardboard box with some food in it and a sports bag with a few clothes inside. On top of the clothes was Dad's hunting knife. Behind that bag was a long leather case. What was in it? Dillon was about to pick it up when he heard the front door slam and saw Dad jogging down the path.

Dillon closed the boot and jumped into the back seat.

"Found my old sleeping bag there, too," Dad said as he slid into the front seat. He threw the three sleeping bags back to Dillon. "At least she didn't chuck that out." He looked angry for a second but then he shook his head. "So, guys, what do you think of my motor?"

"It's cool!" Robbie said.

"Cool!" Dad laughed. "Right, next stop Gardle Head."

Chapter 5

This Is the Wrong Way

They drove towards the centre of town and Dillon leaned over between the front seats to look at all the dials on the dashboard.

"Is it an automatic?" he asked.

"No!" Dad said. "I hate automatics. I love changing gear – reminds me of driving my old armoured car. Screaming round those mountain roads with the towel-heads taking pot shots at us – that was real driving!"

Robbie laughed and pretended to shoot at people out of the window. Robbie loved hearing stories about Dad's time in the army but Dillon didn't like the idea of Dad killing people, especially when he called them 'towel-heads' as if they weren't real people. Sometimes he felt like saying that one of his best friends at school was Gopal and he wore a turban. But he never did. He knew Dad wouldn't understand.

Dillon glanced sideways and saw the tattoo on the side of Dad's head: 'D-A-D'.

"What's that tattoo?" he asked.

"Had it done when I couldn't see you," Dad said. "Made me feel better. Like, people could stop me seeing you but they'd never stop me being your dad. Plus it reminded me of my old man. He had a tattoo on his hand that said 'Dad'."

Dad shook his head and laughed. "That was the hand he used to hit me with. Boy, he had a swipe on him, my old man – he could knock you into the middle of next week! But I loved him to bits. God rest him."

They were coming up to the ring road now. The centre of town was on the right but Dad went to turn left.

"This is the wrong way, Dad," Dillon said.

Dad turned left. "The motorway's this way."

"I thought we were calling at Mum's office," Dillon said.

"What for?"

"You said we could ask her about going –"

"Yeah, but look at the traffic the other way, Dill. It'll take us forever. Anyway, I told you she said it was OK."

"But –"

"But what?" Dad said. "Can't you forget Mum for a change? What about me? Don't I count? This is our time. You, Robbie, me – blokes together."

Dillon didn't know what to say. He wanted to check that Mum really had agreed they could go, but if he said so, it would sound as if he thought Dad was lying.

Luckily, Robbie spoke up. "Can't we just go to say goodbye?"

“Oh not you, too!” Dad snapped. “What’s up with you, Rob? Want Mummy to change your nappy?”

“No.”

“God, you two have gone soft while I’ve been away,” Dad said. “Come on guys – man up here. You don’t want to be wimps, do you?”

“No,” they both mumbled.

“Then grow a pair and make me proud of you!”

Robbie slid down low in his seat and was silent. Dillon sat back and looked out of the window as they sped along the ring road.

Ten minutes later they joined the motorway and they left the city behind. Every mile took them further away from Mum and the safety of home.

Chapter 6

Don't Make Me Angry

They drove in silence.

Most of the time Robbie couldn't stay quiet for more than a few minutes, but now he was hunched down in his seat, not speaking. Dillon knew how he felt – it would be so easy to say something that Dad might take the wrong way.

Dillon watched Dad's hands. They were gripping the steering wheel so tight it looked as if he was strangling it. Then, bit by bit, his hands relaxed and his back started to look less tense.

After nearly half an hour, Dad began to hum a silly song he used to sing to them when they were little kids. Robbie turned his head hopefully and Dad grinned at him and started to sing the words.

"Come on, sing it with me!" he said and they both joined in.

The bad mood was gone as if it had never happened. And there they were, all three of them, roaring along the motorway singing a stupid song about lobsters and bikinis.

Robbie said he needed to stop for a pee and Dad pulled in to the next service station. Dillon was hoping that he'd get a chance to talk to Robbie on his own but Dad went with them to the toilet. Then they all sat together and had something to eat and drink at the café.

"Isn't this great?" Dad said. He put his arms round them both as they got up to leave.

"Can we have some sweets?" Robbie asked as they went past the shop.

"Anything you want, mate," Dad said. He followed Robbie into the shop.

Dillon saw his chance. "See you at the car," he said. Then he ran across the car park and pulled out his mobile phone. He prayed there was a signal here. Yes, it was fine. He could go online and find out the number of Mum's office.

Dillon put the name of the company into the search box. A long list came up. How could there be so many companies with the same name? Then he looked up and saw Dad and Robbie coming across the car park.

No time to get the office number.

Ring anyone then. Andy.

Dillon had just found his number when Dad rushed over to him.

"Who are you calling?" he demanded.

"Andy."

As soon as he said the name he realised his mistake.

"Andy? Who's he?" Dad demanded.

"He's Mum's ..." Dillon wasn't sure what to say. "He's ... Mum's friend."

"Boyfriend, you mean," Dad sneered. "Andy! So that's his name, is it? He's the one who's always coming to the house, isn't he? Staying the night. I've seen him. Looking like he owns the place. Trying to steal my kids from me!"

He reached out and grabbed Dillon's phone.

"Hey!" Dillon yelped.

"Hey, what?" Dad said. "You're with me, right? Your dad, right? Why do you want to talk to some other bloke?"

"I was just going –" Dillon began but Dad cut him off.

"Shut up and get in the car!"

Dillon opened the door and got in.

"Have you got a phone, Robbie?" Dad asked.

"I left it at home."

"Right – get in."

Dillon watched from the car as Dad opened his phone, took out the SIM card and the battery and put them in his pocket. Then he tossed the phone to Dillon and slammed the back door shut.

"Now," Dad said, as he slipped behind the wheel, "perhaps we can have our holiday together without texts and phone calls or anyone knowing where we are."

"You said you told Mum we were going to Gardle Head," Dillon said.

"I told you, this is our time alone. No one else."

"But –"

"I'm warning you, Dillon – don't make me angry," Dad said. He started the car.

As they drove out onto the motorway, he started to sing the song again. But they didn't join in this time.

Dad stopped singing. They drove on in silence.

Dillon thought about what Dad had said. He knew Andy came and stayed sometimes. So that meant he must have been watching the house. He must have hidden outside. All night. In the dark. Watching everything. It was creepy. Really creepy.

And it was obvious now that Dad hadn't gone to see Mum at her office. She had never told him he could take Dillon and Robbie away. And now there was no way they could call her and tell her what was happening.

Dillon could just imagine what would happen when she got back home and found them missing. She would be so worried. It was lucky he had left that note on his bed. She would know where Dad was taking them. And she would know the number of the car.

She would call the police. They would check the CCTV cameras on the motorway. They would soon trace the car and stop them, probably even before they got to Gardle Head.

Then a terrible thought hit him. Suppose they weren't going there? Suppose Dad had only said Gardle Head, but really he was taking them somewhere no one could find them?

Chapter 7
Into the Dark

The silence went on and on.

Dillon kept looking out of the window at all the CCTV cameras they passed. He imagined the police racing after them with their blue light flashing. Imagined them forcing Dad to pull over. Imagined them driving Dillon and Robbie back home.

But mile after mile passed with no sign of that flashing blue light. Then he realised – Mum wouldn't be home yet. Maybe she wouldn't even find the note at first. It could be hours before the alarm was raised. And what if they weren't even going to Gardle Head?

The sun was low in the sky when they left the motorway. The sky turned from orange to blood red and then the light began to fade and Dad turned the headlights on. They stopped at a petrol station and he got out and started to fill up the tank.

Dillon's mind raced. Could he and Robbie jump out of the car and run into the shop to ask for help? What would they say? 'Help, we're being kidnapped'? That would sound stupid and Dad would deny it. Robbie wouldn't understand what was going on and would take Dad's side. Dillon would have to talk to Robbie when Dad went to pay. If he could get Robbie to believe him, they could run and hide at the side of the building. Then, when Dad came out, they could run inside. They wouldn't say anything about kidnap – just get the people to ring Mum.

Dad finished filling the car and put the nozzle back. Dillon got ready to tell Robbie his plan. He'd try not to scare him – he'd just say they needed to speak to Mum.

Then Dad opened the door. "Hey, Robbie," he said. "Want to come in and buy some sweets?"

"I've still got some."

"What about an ice cream, then?"

"Yeah!"

Robbie jumped out of the car and trotted across to the shop with Dad. As they got to the door, Dad looked back at the car. He pointed to Robbie and smiled. What did that smile mean? Did he know what Dillon had been planning and was he smiling because now they couldn't do it? Or was he smiling because he was pleased to see Robbie so happy?

Dillon couldn't tell. It was all so confusing. Maybe he was just imagining the danger. Maybe everything that Dad had said was true. Maybe Dad just did hate texts and mobiles and wanted to go on an adventure without those things.

Maybe Dillon was worried about nothing. Maybe.

Dad and Robbie came back to the car and they drove off again, into the night. Into the dark.

Chapter 8
Our Secret Place

"Nearly there," Dad said.

Dillon looked up. Yes, this was the foot of the long hill that led to Gardle Head.

Dillon felt all his worries fade away. Dad hadn't lied about where they were going. And now Mum would be able to find them if she wanted. Everything was going to be OK.

Dad turned off the road onto a narrow track through the woods. The car lights picked out the tall grass and the little bushes ahead.

"Great," Dad said. "No one's been down here for ages. That's what I love about this place – we always have it to ourselves."

The track got more and more narrow and after a bit Dad steered the car to the right and parked under the trees.

"We'll walk the rest of the way," he said. "Grab the sleeping bags and I'll get the stuff we need out of the back."

Dillon handed the three sleeping bags to Robbie and followed Dad round to the back of the car to get their bags. Dad picked up the box of food and his sports bag and then Dillon leaned in and took out his and Robbie's bags. He spotted the long leather case again.

"What's that?" he asked.

"Oh ... just my snooker cue," Dad said. He closed the boot.

Dillon and Robbie followed Dad as he made his way along the track. Soon the trees stopped and they had to push their way through thick bushes, but Dad seemed to know the right way to go. After a while Dillon could hear the crash of waves in the distance, and then they came out onto the cliff top. Silver flashes of moonlight shimmered on the sea. And the huge blue-black sky sparkled with stars. It was magical.

"Look at it, guys – look at it!" Dad said. "I've been all over the world, but this place is special. And it's ours, our secret place. Hey Robbie, don't get too near the edge – it's a long way down. Right, we'll sleep back there in that hollow next to the bushes. You two strip some small branches off the bushes and lay them on the ground so we won't be sleeping on damp earth."

Dad left them to get on with that while he went into the trees to collect wood for a fire. Just as they were laying the sleeping bags on top of the branches, he came back with a big bundle of wood. He broke off some small twigs and laid them criss-cross on a little pile of dried grass.

There was a bright spark as Dad struck his fire steel and an instant later the grass caught fire. He leaned in and blew. The flames spread to the twigs and then he pulled some pine cones from his pocket and put them on top.

Bit by bit, Dad added branches until the fire was blazing. And now he took out his hunting knife and sharpened the ends of three sticks.

After that he cut three V-shaped branches and fixed them in the ground in front of the fire. Then he took a packet of sausages out of the box. He slid a sausage onto each stick and placed them on the V-branches round the fire so that they hung perfectly over the flames.

In the flickering light of the fire, Dillon saw Robbie's eyes shine with pride as he watched Dad. And Dillon knew how he felt. There was no doubt about it, Dad was good at this sort of thing – a real soldier. Not like Andy, who couldn't hammer a nail in straight and who always had a job lighting a barbecue even with firelighters.

They all sat round and stared into the dancing flames. From time to time Dad twisted the sticks so that the sausages cooked on all sides, and after 20 minutes they were done. Robbie cut some rolls open and Dad put a sausage into each one and covered them with a dollop of tomato ketchup.

"Mmm, that was great," Robbie said, when he'd finished his roll. Robbie had stopped eating meat a while back after he'd seen a TV programme about cruelty to animals. Maybe the fact that he was hungry and that Dad had done the cooking had changed his mind for tonight.

"I'll set some snares tomorrow and catch a couple of rabbits – they'll taste even better than this," Dad said.

They cooked some more sausages, then Dad said they should get some sleep. Dillon lay down in his sleeping bag and looked up at the stars. After a few minutes he heard Robbie breathing deeply next to him and realised he was already asleep. The little kid was so happy to be here with Dad. And why not?

Dillon closed his eyes and went back over the day in his mind. Dad had been fine. True – he'd got angry about the phone and trying to ring Andy, but even then he hadn't really lost it like in the old days. And he'd been funny and warm and loving the rest of the time. It was stupid to be scared of him.

And it was really stupid to think Dad was trying to kidnap them. He couldn't keep them here forever. Dillon could see now why Dad hadn't told Mum – she wouldn't have let him take them away. And that wasn't fair. He was their dad. Why couldn't he have a few days' holiday with his sons?

Sometime during the night, Dillon woke up. Dad was sitting next to the fire looking at him and Robbie.

Dad winked. “Everything’s fine, son,” he whispered. “Go back to sleep.”

Dillon was too tired to say anything. He closed his eyes and drifted off again.

Chapter 9

Don't Be Afraid of Death

It was already light when Dillon woke up. He turned over and saw Dad still sitting next to the fire. He crawled out of his sleeping bag and went over and sat down next to him. The fire was low now, just glowing embers.

"Morning, Dill."

"Have you been awake all night?" Dillon asked.

"Yep."

"Why?"

"Sentry duty," Dad said.

"Aren't you tired?"

"Who cares?" Dad asked. "All that time, I couldn't see you. Now I want every moment I can get. That was the best night I've had for two years, watching my boys sleep."

Dillon's eyes filled with tears and he looked towards the sea so that Dad wouldn't notice.

"It's all misty on the sea," he said, as he blinked the tears away.

"It'll burn off soon. Be a lovely warm day."

At that very moment, just as if Dad had made it happen, the pale sun suddenly glowed behind the mist. Dad was right – it was going to be a lovely warm day.

And then Dillon remembered – the police! Mum was sure to have told them by now. They would be coming to Gardle Head soon. The lovely warm day would be ruined and Dad would know who had grassed him up.

"I won't let them take you away from me," Dad said, and a chill ran down Dillon's back. Had Dad read his thoughts?

“Who?” he asked. His voice sounded a bit funny.

“Your mother and that Andy bloke!” Dad said. “If they think I’ll let some other guy just walk in and try to bring up my boys, they’ve got another think coming.”

He hit the fire with a stick, sending sparks flying into the air.

Dillon didn’t like to see Dad getting angry but he understood. It would be awful for Dad to see Andy move in with Mum and start acting like a new father to Robbie and him.

Dad hit the fire again, but this time the sparks seemed to calm him down. He moved the stick around, stirring the ashes.

“Right, let’s cook breakfast,” he said. “Get the eggs and the pan, Dill. They’re in that box. Thanks. And wake up old sleepyhead there.”

Dad scrambled the eggs and piled them onto slices of bread. Dillon and Robbie were so hungry and the food was so good that they got the giggles as they watched each other stuff it into their mouths. Dad laughed and called them pigs.

When they'd all finished their food, Dad showed them how to look for rabbit runs. He pointed out the trampled grass under bushes, then he took some fishing line from the pocket of his combat jacket and made nooses with running knots. He hung the nooses from branches over three of the runs.

"With any luck we'll snare a couple for supper," he said. "But they won't come while we're here, so let's make ourselves scarce for a few hours – go down to the beach and have a laugh."

There was a deep gorge on the left side of the cliff, with a steep path down to the beach through bushes and short trees. At high tide the waves crashed right up against the cliff, but it was low tide when they got down and there was a long strip of sand and pebbles.

Dad chucked a big branch into the sea and they spent ages throwing stones to stop it coming back to shore on the waves. When Dad got bored doing that, they had a competition to see who could throw stones furthest and then another competition to see who could skip stones the most times. Dad won both competitions, of course, but Robbie nearly won at skipping stones and he beamed when Dillon said how good he was.

They took off their trousers and paddled in the sea, until a big wave soaked them all so much that they decided to take their T-shirts off and go right in. Robbie climbed onto Dillon's shoulders and pretended to wrestle with Dad until they all fell over. The water was cold but they were all laughing so much and having such a good time they hardly noticed it.

When at last they climbed back up to the top of the cliff, they found two rabbits had been caught in the snares. One was dead. It had been strangled as it had tried to get free, but the other was still alive. It struggled as Dad freed it from the snare and held it upside down by its back legs.

"Come on, Dill, put it out of its misery," Dad said. "Use the side of your hand and chop down hard just behind its ears – that will break its neck."

"No, you do it," Dillon said.

"Come on, Dill, don't be a wimp. Kill it."

Dillon hated the idea of doing it but he made himself hit the rabbit the way Dad had said. The rabbit jerked once and was dead.

"Good lad," Dad said. "That wasn't so bad, was it? Robbie, take the other one out of the snare."

Dillon could see his young brother didn't want to touch the dead rabbit but he didn't want to let Dad down either.

"Come on, Robbo," Dad said. "Don't be afraid of death – it's nothing. One minute you're there and the next, you're gone. Nothing."

It was clear Robbie wasn't happy, but he slipped the rabbit out of the snare and gave it to Dad.

"Well done," Dad said. "See, death's nothing."

Chapter 10
A Real Hero

Dad took his knife and began to skin and gut the rabbits. First he cut off their heads and the bottom part of their legs, then he split them open and pulled out their guts. His hands were covered in blood and Robbie let out a groan as he looked at them.

"Just a bit of blood," Dad laughed. He ran his hand across Robbie's face and left a big red smear.

"Dad!" Robbie screamed, as he tried to wipe the blood away with his hand.

Dad just laughed some more and began to pull the skin off the rabbits. When he finished doing that, he took the pan and they all went down to the beach. The tide had come in a long way and the waves had begun to splash the base of the cliff. Dad waited until a wave rolled in and then, as it rushed back out, he stepped onto the beach. He picked up some sand and used it to rub the inside of the pan.

"Sand's better than any washing-up liquid for getting cooked food off a pan, even egg," he said. Then he waded into the surf, rinsed the pan in the sea, filled it with water and waded back to land.

"What's that for?" Robbie asked.

"Gonna boil the rabbits in it," Dad said. "Salt water gets rid of their bitter taste so they'll be sweet and tender when we roast them."

When they got back to the top of the cliff, Dad sent them to look for wood for the fire. They spent a long time searching for dry branches under the trees and along the track. Dillon also loaded his pockets with pine cones and he was pleased when Dad said, "Good lad – learning fast."

They watched as Dad arranged twigs and lit them. Within a minute the fire was burning well, and he piled on bigger pieces of wood.

"It's brilliant, that thing," Robbie said.

"The fire steel?" Dad asked. "Yeah, it's miles better than matches. I'll buy you one for your –" All of a sudden, Dad stopped speaking and a strange look flickered across his face as if he'd thought of something bad. What was it? Was he worried that he wouldn't be able to give them presents when Andy moved in with Mum?

There was an awkward silence while Dad stared into the distance. His mouth was hanging open and he seemed miles away. Lost in his thoughts. Then he was back again.

"Yeah, much better than matches, fire steels," he said. "Even work in the rain. Now, let's get cooking."

He put the rabbits into the water, then made a crater in the middle of the fire and put the pan in it. They sat and watched as the water heated up. Steam began to curl from the water and soon it was boiling. Dad took the pan out of the centre of the fire and stood it on the glowing ashes at the edge.

"They'll simmer away now." Dad smiled at them both.

All day long, Dillon had been worrying about the police turning up. But they would have been here by now if they were coming. That must mean that Mum hadn't called them when she'd found Dillon's note. And that must mean she wasn't worried. So maybe Dad really had gone to see her and she really had said he could take them away.

It would be so great if it was true. They were having such a good time – and Dad ... well, Dad was just amazing. He was so funny and warm – smiling and joking and mucking about all the time. And he was so good at doing everything. What a hero.

He knew Dad had been a real hero in the army and had got a couple of medals, but Dillon had never liked hearing his stories about the fighting and killing. But now they were here and they had seen all the things Dad could do, it made Dillon realise what a great soldier he must have been – someone you'd want on your side if there was any trouble.

They all lay on their backs in the afternoon sunshine. The sound of the waves drifted up to them and Dillon felt good to be here with Dad and Robbie – three guys together.

"What did you get your medals for, Dad?" he asked.

"Oh, most people got the first one – it was just for being over there and not killing the sergeant-major! The other one ... Well, a couple of my mates were trapped in a house and I helped get them out. No big deal."

"I bet it was," Dillon said. "Go on, tell us."

Chapter 11
Two Black Holes

Dad started to tell them how he won the medal and it was like listening to a great adventure story. Dillon lay there with his eyes closed and felt as if he was with Dad on the dangerous streets of a city in the Middle East. And when Dad finished that story, he went on to another. Then another. Talking and talking. Dillon had heard some of the stories before, but they had never sounded so thrilling.

"Enough of that," Dad said at last. He moved the pan with the rabbit in away from the fire and left it to cool on the grass. "Let's go and do a bit of swimming – work up an appetite."

The sun was starting to set and the sea was a wonderful golden colour. The big waves were rolling in and Dad showed them how to catch the breakers just right and body-surf all the way into the shore. It was exciting and a bit dangerous because they could be swept onto the rocks at the base of the cliff. But Dad was always by their side ready to catch them, so they felt safe.

It was dark by the time they went up to the cliff top again. They piled more wood on the fire and sat round it to warm themselves up, then Dad slid the two rabbits onto a long stick.

"They're already nice and tender but we'll just brown them over the fire for a while to give them a bit of extra flavour."

While Dad roasted the rabbits, Dillon could see Robbie looking at them as if they were aliens. It was true that they looked freaky as Dad turned them over the flames, and you could see the big hole in their bellies and their stumpy legs sticking up. Even Dillon wasn't sure he wanted to eat them.

At last Dad pulled the rabbits off the stick and started to tear bits of flesh off them. Poor Robbie looked pale and Dillon was worried he might even be sick.

"Is there anything else for Robbie, Dad?" Dillon asked. "He's a vegetarian and he doesn't like eating meat."

"Oh, do me a favour!" Dad said. "Only girlies are vegetarians. Are you a girl then, Robbo?"

Robbie shook his head.

"You ate sausages yesterday," Dad said. "They're meat. Don't be a girly fusspot. It's only rabbit. I've eaten rat, dog, snake – all sorts. When you're hungry you'll eat anything."

"Isn't there something else he can have?" Dillon asked again.

Dad held out a piece of meat to Robbie, but Robbie just shook his head.

"Starve, then!" Dad said. "Come on, Dill, you're not a sissy, I hope."

Dillon took the meat and ate it. It was really tender and tasty. He looked across at Robbie. There were big tears in his eyes.

"Come on, Rob," he said. "Try it – it's really good. You can go back to being a veggie when we go home. It's different when we're camping, isn't it? It's an adventure. It's like being a soldier, like Dad."

Robbie sniffed and nodded. He wiped his eyes.

"Gonna try, then?" Dad asked. He held out a big piece of meat he'd just ripped off one of the rabbits.

Robbie took the meat. He looked at it, then closed his eyes, put it in his mouth and started to chew.

"Spit it out and I'll knock your block off," Dad said. But Dillon knew Robbie wouldn't spit it out. He was a tough little kid and when he made up his mind to do something he never backed down.

They all ate until they were full. Dad burped loudly. Robbie tried not to laugh but when Dad did it again he giggled and tried to burp, too. Then Dad farted and they all kept trying to burp and fart until they were rolling around on the ground laughing.

"Hey, Dill," Dad said, pulling the car key out of his pocket. "There are a couple of bottles of water and some coke under the driver's seat. Run and get them, will you? I mean, R-U-N, run. Back here in ten, no longer."

Dillon timed himself – dead on four minutes to the car. He opened the door and reached under the seat. As he pulled out the bottles, he saw a ball of paper on the floor near the gear stick. He picked it up and unfolded it.

It was the note he'd left for Mum.

A wave of heat fizzed across his face and down his neck.

So, that was why the police hadn't come.

Dillon put the note in his pocket and closed the door. He was walking away when he thought of something else. He unlocked the car again and went round and opened the boot.

There was that long leather case.

He picked it up. It was heavy.

He undid the strap at the top and opened it.

He found himself looking at two black holes and for a moment he couldn't work out what they were. Then he saw the metal edges and he realised ...

He was looking down the twin barrels of a shotgun.

Chapter 12
Terrible Things

"You took your time," Dad said. "I thought you'd run off or something."

Dillon laughed as if it was a silly idea, but he had thought about it. He'd thought of running away to find a phone and ring Mum to tell her where they were. He'd wanted to do it, but he couldn't leave Robbie.

Dad was staring at him as if he knew the truth.

"It's a long way," he said. "I ran as fast as I could but I had the bottles and –"

"Only kidding – you made good time," Dad said. He took one of the bottles of water and drank from it.

Dillon handed the coke bottle to Robbie who took a long swig, as if he wanted to get the taste of rabbit out of his mouth.

It was getting dark now and a bit chilly. Dillon got his sleeping bag and opened it up. He sat next to Robbie in front of the fire and put the sleeping bag across both their shoulders. Robbie pressed close to him. Dad was looking at them, but Dillon couldn't tell what kind of mood he was in.

"Do you want to come under?" Dillon asked. "It's nice and warm." He lifted the side of the sleeping bag.

Dad shook his head.

Nobody spoke. Far off, an owl hooted. A piece of wood sparked and cracked in the fire.

Dillon tried to make sense of what he'd seen.

The note was obvious – Dad must have found it when he'd gone back into the house before they left. The fact that he'd taken it meant that he didn't want anyone to know where they were going.

OK, so maybe Dad thought that was the only way he could spend time with his sons.

But what about the gun? Why would he want that?

For hunting, of course. Dad had always loved all kinds of hunting.

Then why hadn't he used it to kill the rabbits? Because ... Because it was better to snare rabbits rather than have to pick out loads of pellets before you could eat them? Yes, that was probably the reason.

But why had he lied and said it was a snooker cue? What if it wasn't for hunting? What else could it be for? To protect himself? Who from? The police? No, Dad would never shoot other people. Would he? Well, he must have shot people when he was a soldier. Shot them and killed them. But that was different – it was war.

Dillon looked over the fire and saw Dad staring at him, almost as if he could read his mind. He forced himself to smile. To think of something else. To say something.

"Do you miss the army, Dad?" Dillon asked.

"Yeah, every minute, but I had to give it up, didn't I? She made me," Dad said.

"Mum?"

Dad nodded. "She said she'd leave me if I didn't quit. Said it was no life, with me away all the time, and her working and trying to bring you up. Then she wondered why I got fed up with her. But there I was with no job, no mates. What did she expect?"

"Mum told us you got chucked out of the army," Robbie said.

"I bet she did," Dad said. "She was always putting me down. Trying to make me look small." His voice was bitter, angry, hurt.

Silence. Everyone stared at the fire, thinking. A long time passed.

Then Dad spoke again. "I didn't get chucked out. That's a lie. They just said I needed a break. A rest. They would've taken me back. I know they would. I just needed time to get over things."

"What things?" Dillon asked. Part of him didn't want to know.

"Things you see," Dad said. "Things you do. Terrible things. So much ... blood. Your mates shot or blown to bits. Kids, too. Women and little kids. You can smell the blood ... the smoke ... burned flesh. Terrible things. You're living on the edge all the time. And I went ... funny. It wasn't just me. Other guys ... lost it."

Dillon's blood was pounding in his ears.

"And then you're back here," Dad went on. "Everything's normal. You do normal things. But inside your head you can still see the things you've done. And people don't understand. They say things – little things but ... it just sends you ... you lose it. Your mum pushed me. 'Get a job', 'Do this', 'Do that'. And all I wanted to do was go back. That's the weird thing – I wanted to go back to the war. Be back with the guys."

A cold wind blew across the cliff and stirred the ashes on the fire. The moonlight flashed on the sea. The waves rolled in.

"Go to sleep," Dad said.

Dillon and Robbie went over to the hollow and lay down. Robbie shivered as he got into his sleeping bag. Dillon put his arm round him. After a while he stopped shaking and fell asleep.

Dillon looked across at Dad. He was sitting on the edge of the cliff – a dark shape against the silver sea.

Chapter 13
One Last Day

Dillon watched for what seemed like hours. Dad didn't move and Dillon got more and more worried. Dad was sitting right on the edge of the cliff with his legs dangling over. He'd been so upset – almost crying – when he had been talking. He wouldn't do anything stupid, like throw himself off – would he?

He'd said he'd got better when he was at St Mary's, that he was right as rain now. What did they do to make you better in places like that? Give you pills? Poke around inside your brain? Did it make you better for always?

Maybe Dad was getting ill again. Maybe he still needed help. Mum had never wanted to talk about him when he was in St Mary's. All she'd ever said was that he was locked up and they could feel safe now.

Dillon climbed out of his sleeping bag and walked over to Dad.

"Hello, Dill," Dad said. "Come and sit down."

"It's too near the edge, Dad – come back a bit."

Dad looked down to the waves far below.

"Yeah, long way down. One slip and it would be bye bye." He shuffled backwards.

Dillon sat down and Dad put his arm round him and gave him a hug. "I love you – you and Robbie," he said. "You know that, don't you? You're all I've got – all that matters. You know that?"

Dillon nodded. But he had to say it. "I found the note – the one I wrote for Mum."

"The note," Dad said. "Didn't trust me, did you?"

"Well ... I wasn't sure."

"That's the way," Dad said. "Tell the truth. I like that. There's not enough honesty in the world. War's honest – kill or be killed. The rest of the world's all gone wrong. Money, money, money. Dog eat dog. It stinks. Soldiers are different. They look out for each other. Care about each other. Lay down their lives for each other. Loyal. Brave. That's how I want you and Robbo to be."

The cold wind swept across the cliff top again and Dillon shivered. That gust would have been strong enough to blow someone off the edge if they had been standing there.

"They'll try and break us apart, your mum and her new bloke," Dad said. "Stop us seeing each other. That's not right, is it?"

"No. But if I called Mum and said we're OK, she might change her mind. She must be worried – it's two days."

"A couple of days!" Dad sounded angry. "I had to put up with two years without you."

"I know but if I talk to her –"

"Don't worry," Dad said. "They'll find us soon enough. Then they'll take you away. Put me back in that place."

"They won't," Dillon told him. "You're better now."

Dad shook his head. "They think they can do anything they want. But I won't let them. We'll have one last day together, you and me and Robbie. We'll show them what loyalty is. What real love is. A classic day together – what do you think?"

"Yeah, OK."

"Great. Let's get some sleep."

They went back to the hollow. Dad put his sleeping bag next to Robbie and got into it. Dillon lay down next to Dad.

Dad turned over and stretched out his arms to cover Dillon and Robbie.

So there would be one more day of living like this, then back home. Dad was probably planning to drop them outside the house, but if he came in with them they could tell Mum what a good time they'd had. Maybe when she saw they were safe and well, she would let them go away with him again.

Dillon was worn out and he slipped into sleep with the weight of Dad's arm heavy on his shoulders, as if he wouldn't let him go.

Chapter 14

The Best Shot in the Regiment

Dad was in a hyper mood the next day. Dillon woke up to find him rolling him over and tickling him, and then moving on to roll over and tickle Robbie.

"Wake up, you lazy gits! Rise and shine!"

Dad talked non-stop while he was making breakfast, telling jokes and stories. He was extra nice to Robbie and told him that he would make scrambled egg just for him and that he knew a lot of soldiers who were vegetarian. Robbie smiled shyly as Dad gave him a cuddle and called him "Robbie the Veggie".

Dillon would have preferred to have scrambled eggs like Robbie but he made himself eat the rest of the cold rabbit with Dad because he didn't want to break the good mood. But there was no need to worry – Dad seemed to be determined to make their last day together as good as possible.

They spent the morning on the beach, chasing each other, mucking about and swimming. They built a big sandcastle and then, when the tide began to come in, they started building a wall in front of it to stop the waves. They dug and dug into the sand and piled it really high but in the end the sea won and they watched the waves wash away all their hard work.

In the afternoon they lazed around on the top of the cliff, lying in the sun and chatting. Dad asked them about school and the things they'd been doing for the last two years and he even talked about Mum without getting angry.

They hadn't eaten anything since breakfast and by the end of the afternoon Dillon was beginning to feel really hungry, so he was pleased when Dad asked if they would like fish and chips.

"Yeah!" he said.

"What about Robbie the Veggie?" Dad asked. "Do you eat fish?"

"Yeah, I love it."

"Great," Dad said. "We'll go into Dartley. There's a class chippie there. Then we can go down to that funfair near the pier. Go on the Bumper Cars and the Big Dipper. It'll be a right laugh!"

They walked through the woods to the car and Dad revved the engine and made the wheels spin and skid as they swung round and headed back out to the road. He drove fast, screaming round corners and overtaking everything.

They drove through a small town with the music blaring out from the radio. All of a sudden, Dad screeched to a stop in front of a shop.

"I could murder an ice cream! Here's some money, Dill, nip in and buy us some. Hurry up, I'm parked on double yellows."

Dillon went into the shop and got some choc ices out of the fridge. He took the money from his pocket and held it out to the old woman at the till. She stared hard at him for a moment, then she looked down at the pile of newspapers on the counter.

Dillon followed her gaze and saw the big headline on the front page of *The Daily News* – 'HUNT FOR BOYS'. Under the headline there were photos of him and Robbie. He dropped the money on the counter and dashed towards the exit.

"Hey, stop!" the woman shouted. But Dillon opened the door and ran to the car and jumped in.

Dad roared away from the kerb like a boy racer. Dillon looked back and saw the old woman come out of the shop. Was she taking down the number of the car? Would she phone the police?

"Well, give us the ice creams, dopey!" Dad said.

Dillon handed them out. As he ate his, he wondered what he should do. If he told Dad about the newspaper, it would ruin their last few hours together. In the end he decided to do nothing – they would be going home tomorrow anyway.

When they got to Dartley, they parked on the sea front and walked to the fish and chip shop. The pavement was crowded with holiday-makers and Dillon wondered if anybody would recognise them. He checked the faces of the people as they passed but nobody seemed to notice them.

They sat in the café at the back of the shop and Dad ordered three large cod and chips plus an extra portion of chips, bread and butter, pickled onions, pickled gherkins and cokes. When the girl came over with their order, there wasn't enough room on the table and Robbie got the giggles as Dad mucked around moving things while she tried to fit it all on.

They ate until they couldn't eat any more, and there were still things left over when they got up and left. The man frying the food stopped what he was doing and gave them a strange look as if he had recognised them, but he didn't say anything and Dad didn't seem to notice.

Dad was like a little kid at the funfair. He wanted to go on all the rides and play all of the games. He tried to hook plastic ducks, he threw balls at the coconuts, he tried to knock down skittles, but he was hopeless at all of them. He was brilliant at the Rifle Range, though. He shot down the cowboys as they popped up and he hit the dead centre of the target on the buffalo. He had four goes and each time he won a big teddy bear, but he told the man to keep them.

"Nah, it's not fair on you, mate," he said. "I was the best shot in my regiment. Give them to the next kids that come along. Don't forget."

"Sure," the man said.

They had three rides on the Bumper Cars. Dillon and Robbie shared a car and Dad spent all his time trying to hit them head on. He liked the Octopus and the Dive Bomber rides, too, but the one he really loved was the Big Dipper and they had six goes in a row on that. Then he bought candyfloss for all of them and they wandered up and down looking at everything before Dad had a last go on the Rifle Range. He won again and the man offered him another teddy bear.

"Don't want it, mate. Did you give those other ones to the kids like I said?"

"Yeah."

Dad leaned in and grabbed the man by his shirt. "Don't lie to me or I'll slit your throat."

Dad let go of the man's shirt and gave him a push. The man staggered backwards and almost fell over.

"I mean it!" Dad said. Then he marched away and out of the funfair.

Dillon and Robbie ran after him and when they caught up with him Dillon could see that his whole mood had changed. His eyes stared straight ahead and his lips were moving as if he was talking to himself. He opened the car, slid into his seat, and slammed the door shut. Dillon and Robbie stood on the pavement, shocked, until he opened the window and screamed at them to get in.

This time he drove really slowly through the streets of Dartley. They stopped at traffic lights and after a moment Dad pointed to a Chinese takeaway across the road. There was a big TV hanging on the wall behind the counter and the screen was filled with a picture of Mum, talking to a reporter. Then they showed the same photos that Dillon had seen in the newspaper. There was a shot of the newsreader speaking and then an old photo of Dad before he'd shaved his head.

Dad gave a short, bitter laugh.

"They're after us, boys. But they'll never get us."

Chapter 15

If I Die Before I Wake

They drove back in a cold, deadly silence and as soon as they got to their camp Dad told them to go to bed. They took their shoes off and got into their sleeping bags. Dad walked to the edge of the cliff and stood and looked down at the sea.

"Is he all right?" Robbie whispered, and for the first time he seemed scared.

"Yeah, probably," Dillon said. "But we're going home tomorrow. Don't worry. Go to sleep."

Dillon covered his head with his sleeping bag and smelled the fire smoke and sweat on his clothes. He hadn't changed them in three days. He was just drifting off to sleep when he felt a rough hand shake him.

"Have you prayed? You've got to pray. Get up and kneel – come on, both of you."

They struggled out of their sleeping bags and kneeled beside Dad. He put his arms round their shoulders.

"Say each line after me. Come on."

He started the prayer and they repeated each line after him.

"*Now I lay me down to sleep*
I pray the Lord my soul to keep
If I die before I wake
I pray the Lord my soul to take. Amen."

When they finished the prayer, Dad pulled them close and hugged them.

"Good," he said. "Now go to sleep. And remember, I love you."

They lay down again.

The prayer seemed to have calmed Robbie and he fell asleep fast, but Dillon's mind was racing. He kept his eyes closed while Dad was near them, but when he heard him move away he opened them and watched.

Dad went over to the edge of the cliff and walked up and down. Backwards and forwards, backwards and forwards. Twice he stopped and beat his hands on his head as if he wanted to stop himself thinking. Then he went on walking. Up and down, up and down, muttering to himself all the time. Dillon was too far away to hear what he was saying, but it was like he was having an argument with himself. Then he stopped and bent forward as if he had been punched in the stomach. He started to sob.

It was terrible to hear him like that. It was sad, but more than anything it was scary.

At last the sobbing stopped and he wiped his eyes and stood up straight. Dead straight. Shoulders thrown back. Like a soldier on parade.

Then he came towards them. Silent. Like a ghost. As if he didn't want to wake them.

Dillon closed his eyes.

"I've got to do it, boys." Dad's voice was cold. Dead.

Dillon heard him move away. There was a rustle as he started to walk through the bushes, and then heavy footsteps as he started to run along the track. He was going back to the car. And Dillon knew why.

He was going to get the gun. He was going to kill them.

Chapter 16

Daddy's Going Hunting

Dillon put his hand over Robbie's mouth and shook him awake.

"Shhh, Rob," he hissed. "Listen – you've got to get up. Put your shoes on. Dad's ... he's not well. He's gone to get his gun. We've got to hide. I'm going to take my hand off your mouth but you mustn't make any noise. And you've got to do what I tell you. OK?"

Robbie's eyes looked scared, but he nodded and Dillon let him go.

Dillon thought hard. If they tried to get to the road they might meet Dad coming back. There was only one other way to go – down the steep path to the beach.

It was very dark under the trees on the path and they couldn't go fast. They had got halfway down when there was a roar like a wild beast from the top of the cliff. They froze.

"Dillon! Robbie! Where are you? Dillon! Robbie!"

Dad went on calling their names. He was trying to sound friendly but he couldn't keep the anger out of his voice. The shouts got further away and Dillon knew he was searching for them in the woods. Finally his voice faded away in the distance and everything was quiet. Maybe he'd take the car and go looking for them on the road.

Then they heard Dad's voice again. It was faint but it sent a shiver down Dillon's back. He was singing. The sound grew closer. He was coming back. And now they could hear the song he was singing over and over – the old nursery rhyme:

"Bye baby bunting
Daddy's gone a-hunting.
Bye baby bunting
Daddy's gone a-hunting."

The singing stopped and they both jumped in shock at the sound of the shotgun. Two shots.

In the silence afterwards, Dillon knew that Dad was breaking the gun open and loading it. Then the singing came again from the top of the gorge and he had changed the words.

"Cry baby bunting
Daddy's coming hunting."

Dad was on the path now, singing at the top of his voice.

Maybe they could get behind a bush or a tree and hope he would go past them. Dillon took Robbie's hand and pulled him downhill, looking for somewhere to hide. But there was nowhere.

The singing followed them down.

And now they were at the bottom of the path. Dawn was breaking on the horizon. The tide was in and the waves were splashing the bottom of the cliff.

The singing was getting closer and when Dillon looked back he could see the beam of a torch. Dad was checking every bush by the path.

The only way to go was into the sea. If it wasn't too deep, they could hide behind one of the rocks.

Dillon stepped off the path and found himself waist deep in the water. Robbie jumped in after him and they began to wade towards the rocks. Waves pounded them as they walked and one was so big that it rolled over Dillon's shoulders and he had to hold onto Robbie as it lifted him off his feet.

Dillon looked back and saw the torch beam near the bottom of the path. There was no time to go any further, so Dillon pulled Robbie behind the first rock. It wasn't very big and it only just hid them from view. A big wave was coming towards them.

"Hold onto me tight," Dillon whispered to Robbie, then he grabbed the rock. The wave burst past them and Dillon dug his fingers into the rock to cling on.

The torch beam swept across the water and hit the top of the rock. It stayed there for a moment and Dillon held his breath. Had Dad guessed they were there? Had he seen them?

The light moved to another rock behind them and then to and fro across the waves before it disappeared.

Dillon waited a few minutes, then peeped out. The light from the torch was moving up the path. Dad was leaving.

The tide was still rising and waves were crashing over them but they waited a long time before Dillon decided it was safe. They waded back and pulled themselves out of the water.

Chapter 17
Our Father

The sun was rising but the air was still cold. Robbie was shivering, but Dillon made him wait at the bottom of the path while he went up to the top to check that Dad had gone. He moved slowly and every movement of a bush or a tree spooked him.

At the top of the cliff he peered round. Their little camp was still there – the pile of ashes from the fire, the sleeping bags and their sports bags – but there was no sign of Dad. Dillon held his breath and listened. No sound apart from the distant waves.

He ran down the path to Robbie and told him that they were going try and make it to the road, but that they had to be very quiet.

Robbie grabbed hold of his hand, just like when he was a little kid. Dillon looked at him and smiled.

"Gonna be OK," he whispered.

He was the big brother. He had to keep Robbie safe.

At the top of the cliff, they waited for a moment, then headed towards the gap in the bushes. As they passed the hollow, Dillon looked at their sleeping bags. He was about to look away when he saw one of them move.

He froze in horror and Robbie screamed as Dad threw the sleeping bag to one side and stood up. He was holding the shotgun and he had a strange twisted smile on his face.

"Not bad for a new recruit, Dill, not bad," he said. "Good hiding place behind that rock. Clever to take your time. But you can't fool an old soldier like me."

"Dad, please let us go," Dillon begged. "We want to go home now."

"Without your dad?"

"You can come," Dillon said.

"No, Dill – they won't let us be together. And you don't want to have some other bloke pretend to be your dad, do you? There's only one way to stop them tearing us apart."

"What?"

"It won't hurt, I promise," Dad said. "Dad would never hurt his boys, would he? We've all just got to be brave. It's nothing, death. Happens all the time. I've seen hundreds of people die. It's nothing. Bodies? They're just dead meat. But our souls will fly away and we'll be together forever."

"Dad, no – please."

"I promise you – it'll be easy and quick. Come on – over there near the cliff." Dad waved the shotgun at them and Dillon found himself doing as he was told, as if he was under a spell. He walked towards the edge of the cliff and Robbie followed, still holding his hand.

"That's it," Dad said. "Now I want you to kneel down together."

"Please, no, please," Dillon begged, but Dad waved the shotgun at them. Dillon went down on his knees and pulled Robbie down next to him.

Robbie hadn't made a sound all this time and Dillon knew he must be frozen with terror. He put his arm round his little brother's shoulder.

"I like that," Dad said. "My boys taking care of each other. Don't be scared. We'll look at the sea and the sun and say a prayer, then we'll fly off to a better world. You'll go first but Dad will be with you a few seconds later. And we'll be happy forever."

He kneeled down in front of them, blocking out the light from the sun.

"Come on," he said. "Let's pray together – *Our Father, in heaven ...*"

Dillon's throat seemed to have closed up and he could hardly get a word out. Robbie just moved his lips a couple of times, but Dad didn't seem to notice. He finished the prayer and looked hard at them.

Then he stood up.

Robbie whimpered as Dad lowered the muzzle of the shotgun and placed it against his head.

"No!" Dillon shouted. He pushed Robbie to the side. "Leave him alone!"

The muzzle swung round and Dillon saw the two barrels pointing at him.

"Don't make this hard, Dill."

The muzzle came closer. A ray of sun glinted on the barrel. Then Dillon felt the cold metal on the skin just above his eyes. There was a click as the safety catch was lifted.

This was it. He was going to die. And then Robbie. He couldn't help it – he began to cry. Tears rolled down his cheeks.

"Please, Dad, please! Don't do it. Please. We love you. Robbie and I love you. You're our dad."

There was a tremble in the muzzle. A moment's pressure as Dad pushed forward. Then the pressure stopped and the muzzle moved back.

Dad was looking down at Dillon, puzzled, as if he didn't know who he was looking at.

"Dill?" he said and his voice was croaky. "Robbie?" He shook his head as if he was confused. "What am I ...?"

He stared at them and then stepped back and let out a terrible cry, "Oh my God!"

He twisted the shotgun round and placed it under his chin.

His hand went down to the trigger guard.

His finger searched for the trigger.

Found it.

Squeezed.

There was a flash of light and a splash of red.

One moment he was there. The next he was gone, blown backwards off the edge of the cliff.

Dill crawled forward and peered down.

Dad was lying on one of the rocks. A big wave rolled in and lifted him and carried him forward. His body crashed against the bottom of the cliff, then rolled over and disappeared as the wave drew back.

Chapter 18

In Heaven

Dillon and Robbie were like two robots as they walked away from the cliff top, still holding hands.

They walked along the forest path and past the car.

They came to the road and, without thinking, Dillon turned right and Robbie followed.

They didn't speak, just walked together, hand in hand.

Cars went past but they took no notice of them. They kept on walking. Walking, walking.

Then a car went past and stopped in front of them. There was a blue light flashing on the roof. Policemen got out of the car.

"Where's your father?" one of them asked.

"Our father?" Robbie said as if he didn't understand.

"He is in heaven," Dillon said.

A moment later, there was the sound of running footsteps and Mum's voice. "Dill! Robbie!"

And then she was on her knees, holding them in her arms.

Chapter 19
The Man in the Chapel

The police searched for Dad's body but they couldn't find it. Six weeks later, it washed up on a beach 50 miles south of Gardle Head.

Andy was the one who asked Dillon and Robbie if they wanted to go to the funeral.

"Your mum doesn't want to go and I can understand that," he said. "But if you want to ... it's up to you. Either way is fine."

It didn't take any time to make up their minds. They didn't want to go.

Then, the night before the funeral, Dillon went into Robbie's room.

"Look, Rob, you don't have to come but I've been thinking about Dad and –"

"Me, too," Robbie said.

They went downstairs and told Mum and Andy they had changed their minds – they wanted to go to the funeral.

"Do we have to go alone?" Dillon asked.

"Course not – I'll take you," Andy said.

"I'm coming too," Mum said. She looked at them. "You're right – we have to go."

The chapel was empty when they went in. Dad's coffin was already there and sad music was playing. Robbie took Dillon's hand and held it tight as they walked to the front and sat down. The vicar came in from the side of the chapel and smiled kindly at them. When the music stopped he started to say some prayers.

Just then the door of the chapel opened and a man came in and sat at the back.

The prayers finished and the vicar asked them to stand up for a hymn. Robbie started to cry as they stood up, and Mum cuddled him and stroked the top of his head.

Tears came into Dillon's eyes, too, and he bit his lip to stop them falling. Andy noticed though, and put his arm round him.

"It's OK," he whispered.

Mum tried to sing the words to the hymn but her voice went croaky and the vicar ended up singing on his own. Then they sat down and he read some things from the Bible.

He asked them to kneel and he started to pray again. There was a whirring noise and Dillon opened his eyes. The coffin was sinking down out of sight. Dillon tried not to think about it but pictures of flames kept coming into his head. The coffin was going down to be burned. Dad was going down to be burned.

When the prayers ended and they stood up, the vicar came over and said something to Mum. Then they walked out of the chapel and into the garden.

Robbie was still crying and now Dillon's tears started to fall too. Mum hugged both of them and Andy put his arms round all of them. It felt good to be held like that.

"Let's go home," Andy said at last.

Dillon wiped his tears away as they walked towards the car park.

"Hold on!" a voice called as they got to the car.

It was the man who had come into the chapel. He held out his hand.

"I'm Steve Selby. I was in the army with Scott."

"Oh," Mum said. She shook his hand.

"And you're Kelly," Steve Selby said. "And these two lads are Dillon and Robbie. I'd know you anywhere – Scott was always showing us your photos and talking about you."

"It was kind of you to come, Steve," Mum said.

"I had to," he said. "Scott saved my life in the war. Came back for me and another guy when we were wounded and trapped by enemy fire. Held them off till a chopper picked us up. He was one brave bloke."

Steve looked at Dillon and Robbie. "He was tough as nails, your dad. But a real mate. Someone you could count on to do the right thing. I hope you're proud of him."

Dillon nodded.

Steve turned back to Mum. "I know things went ... wrong ... badly wrong back here, but ... that bloody war messed up a lot of good men. It's like Scott went – I don't know – like he went missing in action out there. Anyway ... I won't forget him."

He stared at the smoke pouring from the chimney at the back of the chapel. "He loved you guys, you know. Loved you a lot."

Then he nodded as if he was agreeing with himself. He flashed a smile at them and walked away.

Dillon and Robbie got in the back of the car, and Andy got in the front. Mum just sat for a long, long time with her hands on the steering wheel. Then she started the car and they drove home.